Contents

Meet the Mystery Mob

Name:

Gummy

FYI: Gummy hasn't got much brain – and even fewer teeth.

Loves: Soup.

Hates: Toffee chews.

Fact: The brightest thing about him is his shirt.

Name:

Lee

FYI: If Lee was any cooler he'd be a cucumber.

Loves: Hip-hop.

Hates: Hopscotch.

Fact: He has his own designer label (which he peeled off a tin).

Name:

FYI: Rob lives in his own world – he's just visiting planet Earth.

Loves: Daydreaming.

Hates: Nightmares.

Fact: Rob always does his homework – he just forgets to write it down.

Name:

FYI: Dwayne is smarter than a tree full of owls.

Loves: Anything complicated.

Hates: Join-the-dots books.

Fact: If he was any brighter you could use him as a floodlight at football matches.

Name:

Chet

FYI: Chet is as brave as a lion with steel jaws.

Loves: Having adventures.

Hates: Knitting.

Fact: He's as tough as the chicken his granny cooks for his tea.

Name:

Adi

FYI: Adi is as happy as a football fan with tickets to the big match.

Loves: Telling jokes.

Hates: Moaning minnies.

Fact: He knows more jokes than a jumbo joke book.

Where's Gummy?

It's Hallowe'en, and the Mystery Mob
are at Dwayne's house. They're all
going out trick or treating – but Gummy
hasn't turned up.

Dwayne Where's Gummy?

Rob He's not here.

Lee Brilliant! You should be
a detective when you
grow up, Rob.

Rob Yeah, well I think I'd make
a great detective.

Adi   OK, let's find out.
Rob, did you know that the police
are looking for a man
with one eye called Sid?

Rob   Really? What's his other
eye called?

Mystery Mob
Doh!

Dwayne   Very funny – but it doesn't
tell us anything that we
don't already know.

Rob What do we already know?

Dwayne That you're a twit
and that Gummy's still missing.

Rob I knew that ... er...
about Gummy, I mean.

Lee Look, we can't wait here all night.
We'll miss all the fun.

Chet OK. Look, you lot go off
trick or treating. Adi and I'll
go to Gummy's house
and find out what's up with him.
We'll ditch our costumes here
and catch you later.

Adi   Gummy's most likely
hiding under his bed
shaking like a leaf.

Lee   Why?

Adi   Think about it. What's going
to happen when he looks
in the mirror to check out
his costume?

Lee   I don't know.

Adi   Well, he's so ugly
he'll scare himself out of his wits!

The Ghost House

Chet and Adi arrive at Gummy's house.
The front door is wide open.

Adi   (shouting) Hello!
        Is anybody home?

There is no answer, so the boys go inside
for a look around.

Chet	Where is everybody?
Adi	I don't know. And why have they all gone off and left the front door open?
Chet	This is just soooo weird. It's like the Mary Celeste.
Adi	Who's she?
Chet	The Mary Celeste isn't a girl. It was a ghost ship. It was found floating out on the sea, but all its crew had vanished!
Adi	Really?
Chet	Oh yes. There was no sign of them at all. But they'd left their dinner on the table – and it was still hot.

Adi	Spooky!
Chet	Too right.
Adi	But I bet we don't find a hot meal on the table here.
Chet	Why not?
Adi	'Cos Gummy would have gulped down his grub before any ghosts got him.
Chet	You're right. He's not called 'Gummy the Greedy Guzzler' for nothing.
Adi	Yikes – look! There's a bloodstain on the sofa.

Chet   You're right!
Or is it tomato ketchup?
I mean, Gummy is
a really messy eater.

At that moment a horrible
screeching sound fills the air.
It makes the boys' blood run cold.

Adi   Arghhh! What on earth
is making that noise?

Chet   I don't know. But whatever it is, it's upstairs.

Adi   (gulping) Do you think it's a vampire?

Chet   It sounds like it.

Adi   And where's Gummy?
Do you reckon the vampire's
taken him up there
so it can drink his blood?

15

Chet It looks that way to me.
Come on, Adi, we've got to
go up there and save him.

Adi But how are we going to
fight a vampire?

Chet No worries. Vampires hate garlic,
and I had garlic bread
for my tea. So I'll just breathe
on the vampire and that'll
fix him!

Adi Great! I hope …

The Haunted Attic

The boys creep up the stairs.
When they get to the top
they don't see Gummy *or* the vampire.
This puzzles them. They scratch
their heads, but then they hear
the screeching noise again.

Chet   The screeching noise
is coming from the attic.

Adi   That must be where the vampire
is ... and poor old Gummy.

Chet   Gummy always says that the attic
in his house is haunted.

Adi   Yeah, but Gummy also says
he's the brainiest
and best-looking kid in school.

Chet   Well, by the sound of it,
          this attic is totally full
          of vampires. So it looks like
          he's finally got something right.

Adi   OK – but how do we get up there?
          Vampires can fly, but we can't.

They see a ladder leaning against
the wall.

Chet   No problem. We can use
this ladder to climb up
to the hatch.

Adi   Fine – but you have to go first.

Chet   Why's that?

Adi   Duh! It's got to be you first
because the vampire's
going to keel over as soon as he
gets a whiff of your stinky breath!

Chet   But what if the vampire bites me before I can breathe on him?

Adi   That's okay. While the vampire's busy with you, I'll nip off back down the ladder and fetch help.

Chet   Oh, you're such a top mate, Adi.

Adi   Hey, don't thank me –
            it's the least I can do.

Chet   You are soooo right there.
            But this isn't helping Gummy.
            Hang in there, Gum.
            We're coming to rescue you!

Chet races up the ladder.
Adi follows him much more slowly.

4

Spooks Alive!

Chet pushes up the hatch. He climbs
into the attic. The attic is dark,
dusty and very gloomy. It has also
gone very quiet. The only sound
Chet can hear is his own heart thumping.
He wishes it would shut up a bit.
The vampire is bound to hear it.
Adi waits on the ladder. He is too scared
to go into the attic.

Adi   Can you see anything, Chet?

Chet   Yes, I can see I'm on my own.
GET IN HERE NOW, ADI!

Adi scrambles into the attic.

Adi   Sorry about that. Er …
it's really dark and creepy
in here, isn't it?

Chet   It sure is, but I can soon fix that.
         I've got my torch.

Adi   Well, hurry up and turn it on.

Chet   All right. Here goes.

The torch light is very weak.
It only makes the shadows seem darker
and scarier.

Adi Oh, terrific. Your torch battery
is nearly flat. It's worse
than useless. And why has it
gone all quiet in here?

Chet I don't know.
Maybe the vampire is …

Before he can say anything more,
a harsh voice screeches *Ex-ter-min-ate.*
Ex-ter-min-ate!

Adi   Arrrgggghhhh! It's not
a vampire. It's a Dalek!
And its voice is coming
from over there in the corner.
Quick, Chet, shine your torch
on it.

The feeble light shows what looks like a white sheet hanging in the air.

Chet   No way is it a Dalek. It's a ghost! Look!

Adi   Oh, blimey. You're right. It *is* a ghost. And it's flying right at us! Run!

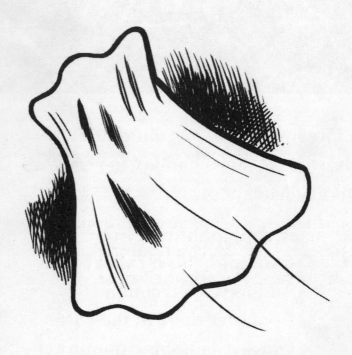

But there is nowhere for Chet and Adi
to run. They are trapped in the
haunted attic. The ghost swoops down
at them. It is screeching horribly.
Is it 'game over' for the boys?

5

Trick or Treat?

The ghost drops on top of the two boys.

Adi   The ghost's got me.
Help me, Chet!

Chet   I can't. The ghost's got me too!

Adi   Hold up. It isn't a ghost –
it's a manky old sheet.

Chet   Yeah, you're right.
And there's something
underneath it that's doing
all the screeching.

Adi   But what is it? And how can it
make the sheet fly?

Chet   Let's grab it and find out.

The boys chase the flying sheet
all over the attic. Chet does a big leap
into the air. He catches hold of the sheet.

Chet   Gotcha!

Ghost   *Ex-ter-min-ate.*

Adi   Go for it, Chet. Pull it down
and see what's under that sheet.

Chet pulls hard on the sheet. It falls
to the floor and a very large
and very angry parrot flies out.
It pecks him hard on the nose.

Chet   Ouch! Dis parrod bid my dose.

Adi   Well, that's because garlic breath
           only works on vampires –
           not parrots.

Gummy's head suddenly pops up
through the hatch.

Gummy   Hi guys. Hey, well done.
You've caught Dalek, my parrot.

Chet   But what's your pet parrot
doing up in the attic?

Gummy He escaped from his cage
when I was feeding him tonight.
He flew out of a window
and up on to the roof.
I've been out in the back garden
trying to coax him down
ever since.

Adi So that's why you didn't turn up
at Dwayne's house.

Gummy   Exactly. Anyway,
Dalek snuck into the attic
through the skylight.
I guess he got tangled up
in that old sheet
and it freaked him out big time!

Chet   Too right. He was screeching
and flapping about like crazy.

Adi   So how come you call him Dalek?

Gummy   'Cos he's always saying,
'Exterminate! Exterminate!'
He learnt that by watching
Dr Who on the TV. Hey –
you didn't think
he was a real Dalek, did you?

Chet & Adi No!

Gummy Oh yes you did.
Well, I guess Dalek's
played a trick on you two
and it's worked a treat!
Now all we've got to do
is trick him into going back
in his cage.

Chet You can do it yourself.
I'm fed up with this – I'm off
to do some real trick or treating!

Adi Me too!

So Gummy has to trick the parrot
on his own. It takes him ages,
but then Gummy is a bit
of a bird-brain himself!

About the author

Roger Hurn has:

- been an actor in 'The Exploding Trouser Company'
- played bass guitar in a rock band
- been given the title Malam Oga (wise teacher, big boss!) while on a storytelling trip to Africa.

Now he's a writer, and he hopes you like reading about the Mystery Mob as much as he likes writing about them.

The haunted Hallowe'en quiz

Questions

1 What has six legs and flies?

2 What do you call the striker in a vampire football team?

3 How do you get the most apples when bobbing at Hallowe'en?

4 What do you call a witch with chicken pox?

5 What do you call a skeleton who tells fibs?

6 What kind of dog does a vampire like best?

7 Why should you never grab a werewolf by its tail?

8 Why did the baby vampire stop drinking milk?

Answers

1 A witch giving her cat a ride on her broomstick.
2 The ghoul scorer.
3 Wear a snorkel!
4 An itchy witchy.
5 A phoney boney.
6 A bloodhound.
7 It might be the werewolf's tail
   but it will be the end of you!
8 Because he wanted something to get his teeth into.

How did you score?

👋 If you got all eight answers correct,
   you are totally ghoul!

👋 If you got six answers correct,
   then you're in high spirits.

👋 If you got fewer than four answers correct,
   then that's a dead loss!

41

When I was a kid

Question Did you ever go trick or treating when you were a kid?

Roger No, my mum wouldn't let me.

Question Really? Why was that?

Roger Because I was wearing a skeleton costume.

Question So what was the problem?

Roger My mum said I couldn't go out because I had no body to go with.

Question Duh! Why didn't you just change your costume?

Roger That's what my mum said. She said I could dress up as Dracula. But I didn't want to be a vampire.

Question Why not?

Roger Because vampires are just a pain in the neck.

Adi's favourite Hallowe'en joke

When do werewolves go trick or treating?

On Howl-o-ween!

How to
trick or treat

 Never go trick or treating on your own.

 Eat garlic before you go out — just in case.

 Take a torch or a glow stick with you.

 Only knock on the doors of well-lit houses, or houses with Hallowe'en decorations in the windows.

 Always go to the front door.

 Always be polite.

 Never go inside a house — even if the person is friendly and invites you in.

Remember tricks must be funny –
never nasty.

 Don't eat any 'treats' until your mum
or dad has checked them out first.
(They will give them back to you again –
honest!)

 Don't get upset if you win first prize
at a Hallowe'en costume party –
and you're wearing your normal clothes!

Fantastic facts about Hallowe'en

1 Hallowe'en is not what you say when you meet someone called Een. It's a very old festival that people in Britain have celebrated for over 2500 years.

2 People in the olden days believed the spirits of the dead came back to visit the living on Hallowe'en. Hmm ... that must be a bit like having your old teacher come round to your house.

3 Trick or treating began when people started leaving food on their doorsteps. This was to stop hungry ghosts from coming into their houses.

4 The word witch means 'wise one'. (Witches are good at maths but their favourite subject is spelling!)

Hallowe'en lingo

Guising This is an old word for trick or treating. It has nothing to do with Guy Fawkes.

Jack-o-lantern This is a hollowed-out pumpkin with a candle inside it. Take care when carving the pumpkin's face. You don't want real blood on your lantern – even if it is Hallowe'en.

Snap apple A Hallowe'en game – not a very grumpy Golden Delicious.

Soul cakes Square pieces of bread with currants given to beggars at Hallowe'en. Hmm … I bet they'd rather have been given chocolate!

Mystery Mob

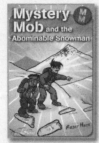

Mystery Mob and the Abominable Snowman

Mystery Mob and the Big Match

Mystery Mob and the Circus of Doom

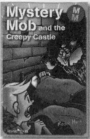

Mystery Mob and the Creepy Castle

Mystery Mob and the Haunted Attic

Mystery Mob and the Hidden Treasure

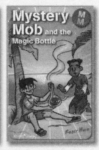

Mystery Mob and the Magic Bottle

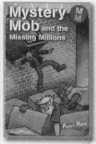

Mystery Mob and the Missing Millions

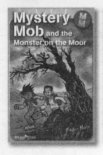

Mystery Mob and the Monster on the Moor

Mystery Mob and the Mummy's Curse

Mystery Mob and the Time Machine

Mystery Mob and the UFO

RISING★STARS

Mystery Mob books are available from most booksellers.

**For mail order information
please call Rising Stars on 0871 47 23 010
or visit www.risingstars-uk.com**

04528237

With special thanks to Anne Marie Ryan
For my aunts and uncles in Florida.

ORCHARD BOOKS

First published in Great Britain in 2018 by The Watts Publishing Group

1 3 5 7 9 10 8 6 4 2

Text copyright © Hothouse Fiction, 2018
Illustrations copyright © Orchard Books, 2018

The moral rights of the author and illustrator have been asserted.

All characters and events in this publication, other than those clearly in the public domain, are fictitious and
any resemblance to real persons, living or dead, is purely coincidental.

All rights reserved.
No part of this publication may be reproduced, stored in a retrieval system, or transmitted, in any form or
by any means, without the prior permission in writing of the publisher, nor be otherwise circulated in any
form of binding or cover other than that in which it is published and without a similar condition including
this condition being imposed on the subsequent purchaser.

A CIP catalogue record for this book
is available from the British Library.

ISBN 978 1 40835 109 3

Printed and bound in Great Britain by Clays Ltd, St Ives plc

The paper and board used in this book are made from wood from responsible sources.

Orchard Books
An imprint of
Hachette Children's Group
Part of The Watts Publishing Group Limited
Carmelite House
50 Victoria Embankment
London EC4Y 0DZ

An Hachette UK Company
www.hachette.co.uk
www.hachettechildrens.co.uk

Series created by Hothouse Fiction
www.hothousefiction.com